THIS WALKER BOOK BELONGS TO:

_____

_____

_____

_____

tick-tock tick-tock tick-tock tick-tock tick-tock tick-tock tick-tock tick-tock tick-

tock tick-tock tick-tock tick-tock tick-tock tick-tock tick-tock tick-tock

For John Browne,
John O'Dowdd
and John Williams
E.B.

For Lucy and William
D.P.

First published 1993
by Walker Books Ltd
87 Vauxhall Walk, London SE11 5HJ

This edition published 1996

2 4 6 8 10 9 7 5 3 1

Text © 1993 Eileen Browne
Illustrations © 1993 David Parkins

This book has been typeset in ITC Garamond Light.

Printed in Hong Kong

British Library Cataloguing in Publication Data
A catalogue record for this book is
available from the British Library.

ISBN 0-7445-4345-2

ock Tick-Tock

Written by
Eileen Browne

Illustrated by
David Parkins

WALKER BOOKS
AND SUBSIDIARIES
LONDON • BOSTON • SYDNEY

Skip Squirrel and her mum
lived in a tree house
with bouncy squirrel chairs
and a squirrel cuckoo clock.
The clock went,

Tick-tock ... tick-tock.

And the cuckoo popped
out and sang,

Cuckoo

at one o'clock.

Cuckoo, cuckoo

at two o'clock.
And at four o'clock
it sang,

Cuckoo

four times.
"I love that clock,"
said Mum to Skip.

One afternoon Mum had to go out.

Tick-tock ... tick-tock.

"I'll be back at four," she said.

"And NO JUMPING ON THE CHAIRS!
Something might get broken."

"OK," said Skip.

They rubbed noses goodbye,
and with a flick of her tail,
Mum was gone.

"Hi-ya!" Skip's friend, Brainy, leapt into the tree house. Skip was so pleased to see her, she FORGOT what her mum had said… She JUMPED ON A CHAIR! So did Brainy.

Boing! Boing! They bounced up and down.

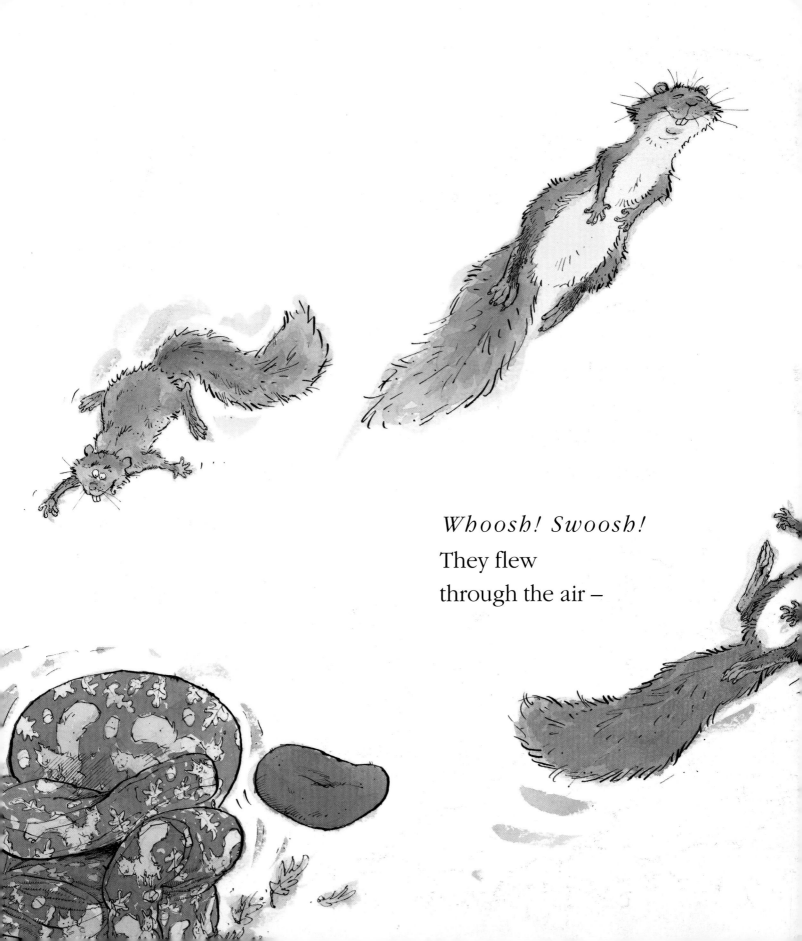

Whoosh! Swoosh!
They flew
through the air –

CRASH!
into the cuckoo cloc.
Tick-tock …
tickerty-tockerty …
CLUNK!
The cuckoo clock stopped.
"Oh, no!" cried Skip. "It's broken.
Help! Mum will be back at four!"
"Don't panic," said Brainy.
"Relax! We'll take it to Weasel.
She mends things."

They ran through the woods to Weasel's.

"Can you fix this clock?" asked Skip.
"Let's see," barked Weasel, and opened it up.
"Aha!" she said. "This clock's got a puncture!"

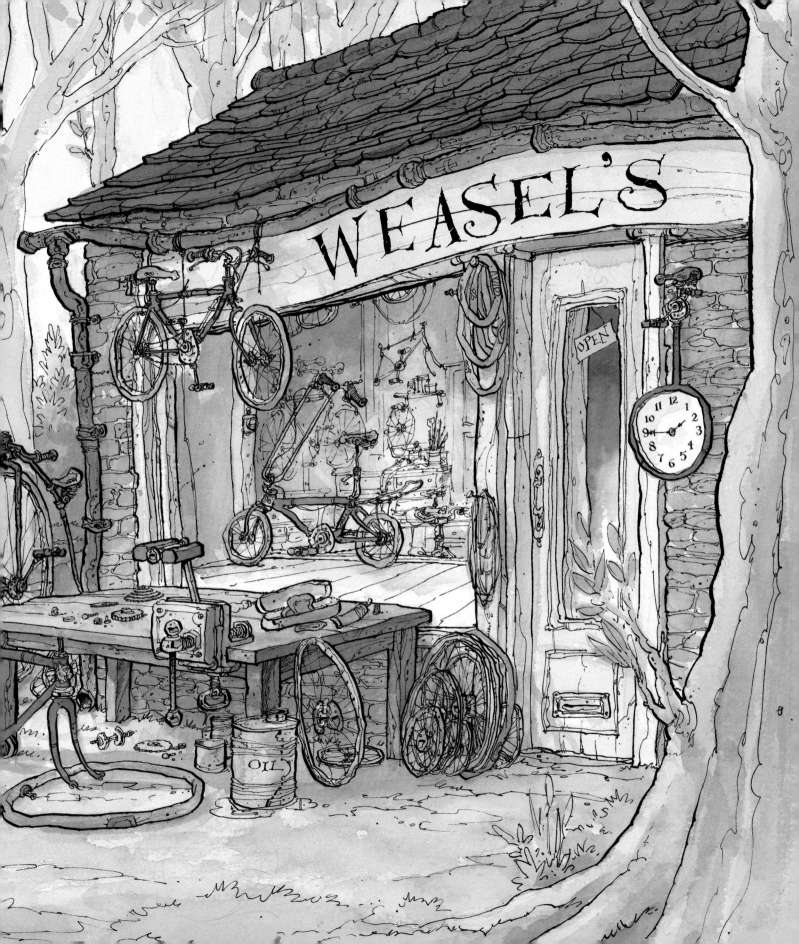

Weasel glued on two patches
and pumped in some air.
"Soon have it on the road again,"
she said. "I'll just oil the chain."

Drip ... drip...

Whirr ... whirr...

The clock started!

Tick-tock ...

tickerty-tockerty ...

CLUNK!

The cuckoo clock stopped.

"Oh, spanners!" said Weasel. "I can't fix it."

"Oh, NO!" cried Skip. "It's two o'clock.
Mum will be back at four!"

"Don't flap," said Brainy. "Calm down!
We'll take it to Hedgehog. She mends things."

They raced through the fields to Hedgehog's.

"Can you fix this clock?" asked Skip.
"I'll try," snuffled Hedgehog.
She looked underneath.
"Oooh," she said.
"This clock's worn out.
It needs new soles!"

Hedgehog stuck on some soles,
polished the front and fitted red shoelaces.
"Soon have it back on its feet," she said.
"I'll just hammer this nail in."

Tap ... tap...
Whirr ... whirr...
The clock started!
Tick-tock ...
tickerty-tockerty ...
CLUNK!
The cuckoo clock stopped.
"Oh, flip-flops!" said Hedgehog. "I can't fix it."
"Oh, NO!" cried Skip. "It's THREE o'clock.
Mum will be back at four!"
"Don't worry," said Brainy. "Keep cool!
We'll take it to Owl. She mends things."

They rushed through the trees to Owl's.

"Can YOU fix this clock?" asked Skip.
"Of course," said Owl.
"Tu-whit-tu-whoo,
 I LOVE mending clocks.
 Let's have a look."

"What's this?" said Owl.
"Puncture repairs? Bike oil?
Soles? Shoelaces?"
She pulled off the patches
and cleaned up the oil.
She unstuck the soles
and untied the laces.
Then she tinkered
for ages …
and ages …
and AGES…

Whirr … whirr…
The cuckoo clock started!
Tick-tock … tick-tock …
tick-tock … tick-tock…

"It's working!" cried Skip.
"Yes," said Owl.
"Now, let's hear it
cuckoo!"
"No time," said Skip.
"Thanks, Owl.
But I MUST get this
clock back by four."

Tick-tock ...
tick-tock...
"Don't drop it,"
said Brainy, as they
ran back to Skip's.

Tick-tock ...
tick-tock...
"Don't slip,"
said Skip, as they
climbed up her tree.

Tick-tock ...
tick-tock...
Carefully, they
hung the clock
back on the wall.

It was ONE
MINUTE to four.
"Phew!" said Skip.
She flopped
in a chair.

"See you later!"
said Brainy, and
waved goodbye.

Tick-tock ... tick-tock ...
tick-tock ...
   tick-tock...
      "Hello–o!
      I'm home!"
      Mum Squirrel
      jumped in and
      gave Skip a hug.
      "Have you been
      good?" she asked.

But before Skip
could answer, the
cuckoo popped out
of the clock and
   sang ...

TU-WHIT-tu-whoo,
TU-WHIT-tu-WHOO,
TU-WHIT-tu-WHOO,
TU-WHIT

- TU - WHOO!

tick-tock tick-tock tick-tock tick-tock tick-tock tick-tock tick-tock tick-tock tick-tock tick-

MORE WALKER PAPERBACKS
For You to Enjoy

NO PROBLEM
by Eileen Browne / David Parkins

Mouse is sure she can put together Rat's construction kit – NO problem!
But as she – and her friends – soon discover, it's not as simple as it seems!
The book includes a cut-out model to make.
"A fascinating and vividly illustrated story." *Books For Your Children*

0-7445-3632-4   £4.99

WHERE'S THAT BUS?
by Eileen Browne

Rabbit and Mole are waiting for the bus, but there's always something
to distract them at the vital moment… Young children will love
the joke of being one up on the characters.

"A lovely book with bold pictures and clear entertaining text." *Books for Keeps*

0-7445-3608-1   £3.99

HANDA'S SURPRISE
by Eileen Browne

As Handa walks, a variety of animals help themselves
to the different fruits in the basket on her head.

"Rich in the colours and space of Africa … the pictures are so sensual
the reader can almost smell the various fruits that Handa is carrying…
A delight to read aloud or for beginner readers to read for themselves;
it is beautifully produced and a joy to handle." *The School Librarian*

0-7445-3634-0   £4.50